j
Timm, Peter Gerald
Attack of the cat

3 d 4

DO NOT REMOVE
CARDS FROM POCKET

(Prime Time Adventures)

THE ATTACK OF THE CAT

By Peter Gerald Timm

Illustrated by Len W. Meents

 CHILDRENS PRESS, CHICAGO

Library of Congress Cataloging in Publication Data

Timm, Peter Gerald.
 The attack of the cat.

 (Prime time adventures)
 SUMMARY: As he patiently stalks a mountain lion,
Ed thinks about the tragedy the killer cat has
brought to the valley.
 |1. Pumas—Fiction| I. Meents, Len W.   II. Title.
PZ7.T484At |Fic| 80-27359
ISBN 0-516-02101-X

CONTENTS

CHAPTER **1**

THE ATTACK

Ed walked through the trees. He had been home a few weeks. Today, he went hunting. It was late afternoon. Spring was early. Snow was in spots on the ground.

He carried the shotgun on his shoulder. He could pull it forward and fire fast. Maybe I'll find something for dinner, he thought.

He didn't see the mountain lion. It was on a flat rock above him. It moved from foot to foot. It was close to the ground. It was getting set to attack. Then, it was still. Ed walked on toward the flat rock. A soft wind came through the trees.

Ed didn't know what hit him. The cat jumped ten feet through the air. It hit him like a big rock. Shock made him pull the trigger. The gun went off next to his head. His ears rang. But it was close to the cat's head, too. It was frightened off. Ed got a look at it, running into the woods, as he hit the ground.

He couldn't breathe. The cat was big. It had hit him hard. He thought he would pass out. Then, he felt the sharp, hot pain.

He had a thick shirt on. His left arm was bloody. The shirt was torn away at the shoulder. A wide, bloody gash was near his neck. Now, blood came through his shirt in front. Was he going to die?

Get up, he told himself. What if it comes back? The thought made him get up. Blood ran down his left arm into his hand.

"The shotgun," he said out loud. He reached for it with his left hand. The pain made him scream. He fell.

He knew it was a mountain lion.

Boy, it must be big, he thought. Big as the one that killed Shorty.

"Why did I come back here?" he said to himself.

"Shorty." The pain made him call out the name of his dead friend.

Shorty had been dead for three years. He was killed fighting a mountain lion in this same place. Ed had seen it all. Now he was back. He had stayed along the stream below, hunting. He told himself he was never going to come back here. But he kept thinking of that fight three years ago. And he came back. It was wrong. Now, he was finished, torn open by an animal.

For three years he was in the war. In France and Germany, he was never hurt. Now he was home. Back with his dad to work with their cattle and build the business. If he didn't die.

He knew he couldn't make it back to the truck. He had left it below in the valley. The shotgun. He had to get to the shotgun. The cat might try to jump him for the kill.

"Get up," he said to himself. He forced himself up. He looked up at the flat rock. The attack came from there. Nothing. The cat was staying away. He looked at his hand. Blood

was still running between his fingers, dropping onto the ground.

He wanted to lie down. Just pass out, he told himself. It would be easy. Go to sleep and never wake up. But, he reached for the shotgun. Pain burned in his shoulder. He grabbed the end of the shotgun with his left hand. But he knew he couldn't lift the gun to fire. If he could rest it on something, he could still pull the trigger with his right hand. The rocks. He could lie down behind a pile of rocks. They were all over. With the gun on a rock he could aim and fire. If he missed, the noise would frighten the cat off for good. What if it didn't?

"The well," he cried out.

That was it. He could get into the well. Safe on all sides, the cat couldn't get at him. He could wait for it to get close. Wait until he couldn't miss. Then, a clean shot.

Three years ago, Shorty had made the well to keep their food in. They hunted and fished up here, camping out for days at a time. Shorty had piled rocks on top of each other in a circle. He made a round stone wall about four feet

high. They covered their food in the well with rocks. Animals couldn't get at it when they were away.

Ed moved toward it. He pulled the gun in his left hand. It was wet with blood. It slipped out of his bloody hand. He didn't feel it slip away.

The sun was setting. He didn't want to be here when it got dark. Someone will come looking for me, he told himself. Did they know

another cat was around? Maybe not, he
thought. What if they think I'm camping out
tonight? They won't expect me back.
    "Get to the well. Go," he said out loud.
    He felt safe as soon as he got there. With his
right hand, he grabbed the rock wall. He was
going to use the shotgun as a cane. He could
push himself up with his other hand. Then he
saw that he had dropped the gun.
    Just then, the cat screamed. Ed went cold. It
was worse than anything he had heard. It
sounded like the animal was in pain. But Ed
knew it wasn't. Anger, that's what it was, he
thought. He was mad at himself for dropping
the gun.
    Ed almost gave up. He could never make it
back to the shotgun. He was close to passing
out. And the cat was still out there in the trees.
Waiting.

CHAPTER **2**

THE SAME CAT

A mountain lion looks for the weak one, Shorty once told him. He picks the animal that's hurt and can't keep up.

That's me, Ed thought. Weak. About to be killed by a mountain lion. He grabbed the rock wall of the well. He pulled himself up, hurting with pain. It almost knocked him out. He fell into the well. But the bottom was still covered with snow. It broke his fall.

He lay still. His head cleared. The snow! He began putting it into his mouth. The snow felt good in his mouth. Cold and good, it ran into his throat. What did they tell him in the army about bleeding? Something cold could stop it. He opened his shirt. He packed his shoulder with snow. At first, nothing happened. But Ed kept packing it on. His shoulder finally felt numb from the cold.

He sat with his back against the stone wall. The well wasn't big enough for him to straighten his legs. He knew what he had to do next. A large flat rock was on top of the wall. It had been used to cover food in the well. If he turned on his side, the rock would be big enough to cover his head and shoulders. He had to pull it down on himself. Then, he could pull in more rocks and cover the rest of his body. But he would wait until he had to. For now, he would listen and watch for the cat. He could see all around him through the cracks in the stone wall.

He looked at the blue sky. The sun would go down soon. Ed liked this time of the day. Now and then a bird sang. Not much, just a few notes. A soft wind came and went. Then, everything was still.

High overhead Ed watched a bird. It sailed in the sky. The wind held it. It hung in the air a minute. The wind let it go. Then, it sailed again.

Ed began to get a feeling of peace. Always, it had been peaceful here. That's why he and Shorty had camped here. It was a large clearing, like a table top placed in the side of the hill. Below was the valley. From here, they could see for miles along the valley. The stream where they had fished was just below.

Sometimes they just sat on the flat rocks, looking into the valley. The rocks were round, like giant pancakes piled on top of each other. Shorty had spotted a lion from there. It was the lion that killed him. It was hard to believe. That was three years ago. It was still fresh in Ed's mind. He and Shorty had been watching the valley below. Some wild horses were feeding on the spring grass. The lion was watching them, too.

"Look." Shorty pointed. Ed saw the cat. It moved slowly. It stayed close to the ground. It stopped. Waited. Moved closer. Slowly.

"He will never catch them," Ed said. "They will spot him and take off. They can outrun him."

"No," Shorty pointed again. "That one, off to the side, it's hurting. Looks like a bad foot. The cat's got his eye on him. It's the weak one."

Just then the horses took off. It was as if

each horse had seen the cat at the same time. It was coming at them. But it was not running at top speed, yet. The horses looked like they were flying. If it were not for the dust, Ed would have said they were flying.

All but one. The one with the bad foot. Shorty was right. He could not keep up. He was way behind the others. The cat knew. Then, Ed saw a sudden change in its body. It had been running easily. Now, its rear legs really drove it forward. Front legs shot out in front. The legs came together under it, driving it faster and faster. It was one movement. Its body was a straight line.

It hit the horse in the neck. Its claws dug in. The horse tried to keep its legs going but couldn't. It went down, head first. The cat jumped off when it fell. Now, it hit the neck again. Flat on its side, the horse kicked once at the air. Then it was dead.

In the well now, Ed thought back on it. It seemed like yesterday. Today, three years later, a cat is hunting me, he thought.

As if the cat were reading his thoughts, it screamed. Ed grabbed the flat rock. He pulled it into the well. It fell on him, but he barely felt it. He pulled in more rocks from the stone wall.

Not too fast, he said to himself. The snow packs had stopped the bleeding. He didn't want to start it again.

He looked through a space between the rocks in the wall. The sun was setting. It was almost dark in the clearing. Ed knew the cat was out there, but it still frightened him when he saw it. The sun was still shining on top of the pancake rocks.

There it was. It was still. Its head up, ears up, tail not moving. It was watching the well.

Ed could see everything about it. A dirty yellow coat. Black spots near its mouth. Then he saw the scar on its chest. At first he couldn't believe it. His heart missed a beat. The sun was shining on the scar.

"It's the same cat," he said out loud. "The cat that killed Shorty. It's back!"

The cat stood still in the setting sun.

The size alone told him it was the same cat. It was bigger than most, almost eight feet long. The scar told him the rest. Shorty gave it that scar three years ago. Knife in his hand, he had torn the cat's chest. But not deep enough to kill. Then they had the fight Ed couldn't forget.

Now, the cat was back. From the rocks, it watched the well.

Ed dug a hole in the snow. He put his left shoulder in the hole. Then he packed more snow near his neck. He pulled more rocks into the well, covering the rest of his body. He felt rocks under him. They dug into him. He reached to pull them away. Cans! Not rocks under him. Cans of food and a box of shotgun shells. They had left them here three years ago.

He could use the bullets. He put one in his teeth and bit into the end of it. The gunpowder in the shell would burn. He got the shell off the bullet. Then another one. He put the gunpowder into a small pile two feet from his face. Matches. He reached in his shirt pocket for them.

Ed pulled the round flat rock over his head and right shoulder. Through the cracks in the wall he looked for the cat. It was walking near the well. Now and then it stopped and looked. Then it jumped and was on top of the wall. He could hear it. He didn't move. The cat put its front legs on the rock that covered Ed.

Ed lit a match and dropped it into the gunpowder. The second his hand came out, the cat went for it. It hit the gunpowder as it went off in a white flash. The cat jumped away. White smoke flew out of the well.

Ed pounded on the ground. He laughed out loud.

"How do you like that, cat?" He laughed again.

Ed put another bullet in his teeth. He opened it. He made another pile of the black gunpowder, this time on top of the wall. Watching him, the cat was still. The gunpowder flashed again. The cat's ears went up. Then it walked off into the trees.

"And don't come back," Ed shouted. But he knew it would. He kicked the rocks off his feet and legs. He was tired, ready to pass out. It was getting dark. He had to sleep.

"Don't go to sleep," he said out loud. "Stay awake. It's going to come back."

He opened more bullets. But he knew he had to sleep. Besides, he could take care of himself. He put the gunpowder right next to his face. Just don't open your eyes when you light it, he told himself. He was ready. He pulled the flat rock over his head and went to sleep.

CHAPTER **3**

JACOB SHORT, REMEMBERED

For a while it was very dark. Then the moon crossed over the clearing. The pancakes stood high and dark in the moonlight. There was darkness in the trees behind. Sky, full of stars. Far away, an animal barked. The clearing was still.

Ed woke. He was very cold. The moon was high. Its light was cold and white in the clearing. His shoulder and neck burned. He was stiff and in pain. Get out of here, he thought. Walk back to the truck. No. That's crazy. He was safest in the well. Someone will come in the morning.

He pushed the rock off and sat up. It was cold. He couldn't stop shaking. A fire would be good. But there was nothing to burn. The gunpowder didn't burn long enough. It went up in a flash. No good for warming himself.

14

Suddenly, he heard a crashing sound. His head went up. He looked. Nothing. Then the smell of a skunk came into the well. An animal had gone after the skunk. That animal was paying for it now, Ed thought. He hoped it was the cat. The smell made him sick. But he stopped thinking about the cold.

Ed wondered why the cat came back. He wished he could ask Shorty. He wondered how Shorty had known so much about animals and the land. A good man, Shorty had been.

The first time Ed saw Shorty, he was in old Sam Parker's truck. It was in the spring, three years ago. Sam had picked him up somewhere. Told him he might get work from Ed's dad. He told him Ed and his dad lived together. Ed's mother died of the fever, he said.

Shorty climbed out of the truck with an old bag. He thanked Sam and the old man drove off.

They had looked at each other for a minute. Shorty's face was brown and worn. But it was friendly.

"You need something to eat?" Ed asked him.

"Yes," and added, "but I'll work for it."

"My name's Ed Winner, what's yours?" Ed asked.

"Jacob Short. People call me Shorty."

He was anything but short. He must have been six-foot-two. Thin but not skinny, he looked like a man who always worked outside.

He helped Ed shoe the horses. He knew what he was doing, all right.

At dinner he didn't talk much. He said he had worked in the oil fields, been a cowboy, and a few other things. But oil was the business he knew best. Then the hard times came. Everyone was thrown out of work. He took a job where he could find one.

After dinner, Ed's dad said, "I'll give you work, Jacob Short. Can't pay you. But you'll get food and a place to sleep. If times get better, I'll pay you. Or, you can move on. Up to you."

Shorty said OK and thanked him. That was it. For Shorty, it was time to get on with things and not look back. That summer, the cat would kill him.

They worked together. They were close friends. Shorty was a lot older, but he never acted like Ed was a kid.

Ed's dad had sheep back then. So did the others. No one was rich. They hoped things would get better. More water and grass for the sheep. Easier winters. The land didn't give them a lot.

Summer came. Shorty and Ed fished when they could. They had first spotted the cat from here. From the pancake rocks, the day it killed the horse. Off and on, people in the valley had hunted the cat that summer. Everyone knew it would go after the sheep. They found a few dead sheep. But no one saw the cat for a while. Then it came back.

It was the worst thing that ever happened. The cat killed old Sam Parker's grandson. The boy and his sister lived with their grandparents.

The kids had been playing. They were close to some sheep. A lamb had left his mother. The boy was holding it. The little girl tried to

get on its back. But the small thing's feet fell in under it. They laughed and tried again. The cat was watching them.

The boy spotted the cat. He threw a rock at it. The cat ran off. He threw another rock. The cat ran into the trees.

The kids got tired of the game. They started to walk home. They were near their house. Then they heard the lamb cry. Both ran back. The cat was pulling the lamb through the bloody grass. It was dead.

The boy went to drive the cat away. It was the wrong thing to do. The cat jumped at him. The boy went down under him. The little girl screamed.

Sam got to him first. He picked him up by the shoulders. The boy's head just fell to the side. His neck was broken. Sam fell to the ground. He started beating on the ground.

"It's a man eater," everyone was saying up and down the valley. "It's a killer cat."

They were thinking of more than just the sheep now. Little kids were kept inside. A good thing everyone carried a shotgun. They thought they saw the cat every place. Now and then a shot was fired.

In fact, no one had seen the cat up close. The little girl saw it. But she still couldn't talk about it. So no one could say *what* it looked like.

"It doesn't matter," Ben Kincaid said. "We just shoot a mountain lion. Two, three, if we see them."

Ben had started the hunting party. It was the same day the boy was killed. He got the word out. By the next afternoon, a group of men had come on horseback. They planned to look through the hills along the valley. The first to spot the cat was supposed to fire his shotgun. The rest would come on the run. They would follow the cat until they could shoot it.

"Let's hear just two shots," Ben said. "The shot that calls us after the cat. And the shot that kills it."

They rode out late that summer day. Too late, Shorty said. He thought they should start the next morning. More daylight that way, he said. But he rode with the rest of them.

Sam Parker got his shotgun and rode, too.

"It isn't right," Ed told Shorty. "Sam should be home."

But Sam didn't think of them. He was in his own world, now. He kept seeing the little boy's broken neck. The animal was something bad and mean. It must hate me, Sam told himself.

"Why would it do that to me? Why take my grandson?" he asked Ed.

Ed started to worry about him. Sam was talking strangely. "Take it easy, Sam," he said.

They decided to ride all night. Ben said they would stop sometime the next day.

"Tonight we will keep the cat moving in front of us," he said. "Keep pushing him. Make him shaky. Maybe he will show himself."

Some of the men didn't like it. "Ben, in the dark we could end up shooting each other," one man said.

"Don't shoot at anything," Ben answered. "Just fire in the air if you want the rest of us to come. It will be too dark to get a clean shot at the cat."

"OK. We'll just keep pushing him," someone said.

They rode into the hills. Ed stayed at Sam Parker's side. Sam held his shotgun across the saddle.

"Sam? No shooting. You heard. Right?"

He answered very softly. "I won't shoot anyone. Just that wild animal."

Ed didn't like this. He kept one eye on Sam, and one eye watched for the cat.

"I'm getting too old for a night in the saddle," Ben said. He rode just in front, with Ed's father. Ed heard them talking.

John Winner said, "Yes, but we better ride along. Keep them from shooting each other."

Both men had lived here all their lives. They got the land from their fathers. Before that, their grandfathers had come. Over the years, each family had worked hard—worked hard to control the land. The cold winters, the burning summers, right up to the present.

"Here we go again, John. Hunting a cat," Ben said.

"We can't be sure it's only one," his friend answered. "Remember about ten years ago? We hunted packs of them."

They had talked about that. Some lions had killed three sheep one night. The men hunted for a week. It was very cold. They shot four of the lions. Then, a year later it was the same. Finally, they drove the cats out of the valley. It took years.

They talked about the winters. Ed thought of one winter. They had been snowed in. The sheep couldn't dig through the snow. They couldn't get to the grass. And the men couldn't get food out to them. Finally, it began to get warm. They found many sheep dead.

"I don't know," Ben said. "Seems like you can't win."

Summer was the worst for some people. Those times that the water dried up. Some bad summers they lost almost half their sheep.

"And if that isn't enough," Ben said, "the Indians steal the sheep."

Ed waited for his father to speak. John

Winner said nothing. He knew Indians took the sheep. He told Ed they had to. They didn't have enough to eat. Besides, they took only what they needed, he said.

He spoke to Ben. "We're winning," he said, "but it takes time. My granddad had nothing to eat one winter. And my father had to fight the cattle men. Bloody fights they were," he said.

"I guess we are better off," Ben said. "But you have to keep at it. You can't rest."

"That's what happens on this land," Ed's father said.

"Yes, so let's get that cat," Ben said.

CHAPTER **4**

THE HUNT

They rode into the hills. Ed and Shorty rode together. But they kept Sam Parker with them. Ben asked them to keep an eye on Sam. He was acting funny, Ben said.

It was soon dark. Their horses climbed. The ride was harder now. And the night was cold. A white moonlight made things look strange. Away off, an animal barked and cried. The riders kept on.

Ed was jumpy. He worried about Sam. He felt that the darkness held something. Something bad for all of them. He had seen the cat go after the horse. He had seen the speed of the kill. He wished they could just listen. But it was more than the cat. Something worried him. He couldn't explain it.

Just then, something ran through the trees. Ed jumped and brought his shotgun up to fire.

Nothing. They had frightened some small animal. Ed looked at Sam. The old man was just looking in front of him. He had not heard a thing! Ed thought how he hated the cat. The cat had brought them out there. It could hit one of them in a second. And Sam Parker would be no help. He was shaky, at best.

Shorty was in the lead. Now he stopped and held up his hand. Ed brought his horse alongside Shorty's.

"What is it?" he asked.

Shorty just sat still, listening. His eyes studied the darkness.

"You hear something?" Ed asked again.

"I heard a voice."

Ed heard nothing. "Maybe one of the others."

"No," Shorty said, "none of them is close to us. Listen."

They heard nothing. They were near the top of a hill. Shorty got off his horse. He whispered to Ed. "Tell Sam to watch the horses. You and I will walk to the top, OK?"

"What if the cat's near here? It might go for the horses." Ed was worried. "Besides," he said, "what about Sam?"

Shorty looked at Ed. "We have to go look. Someone is on the other side of that hill. And he didn't come here with the rest of us."

Ed took their horses to Sam.

"Sam, we are going to have a look. Take care of the horses. You'll be all right."

Ed tied the horses to a tree. Sam sat on the ground and looked up the hill.

Ed and Shorty walked. They stopped every so often and listened. They didn't hear a sound. They kept on up the hill. At the top they sat. The moon was hidden. Down the other side of the hill it was very dark. They tried to see.

Ed spoke. "Shorty, you sure you heard a voice?"

Shorty looked at the sky. The moon was

coming out again. Shorty pointed at a place below.

Ed saw it then. It looked like a man. Then it was gone.

Shorty whispered, "Let's get closer."

Slowly, carefully, they made their way down the hill. They saw it again. It moved its arms. Then it went down to the ground.

Shorty called out. "Who are you?"

It was gone in a second. Ed and Shorty ran to the spot. They looked in the grass and trees. It was gone, all right. Shorty went back to where they had seen it. He lit a match, then another. He was studying the ground.

"What do you see?" Ed asked.

"The footprints of a big cat."

Ed looked. "What about a man's footprints?"

"No, just the feet of a cat," Shorty said.

Ed spoke fast. "You mean that thing was not a man? Shorty, it was a man."

Or was it? Ed was shaking. He held his shotgun and looked into the dark.

Shorty said, "Let's get the horses. Maybe we can find him." He started back up the hill. Ed was right behind him.

They were almost up the hill. Shorty stopped a few feet from a tree. He looked up. He was going to be careful. But there was nothing up in the tree.

Just then, part of the tree popped open. Pieces of wood flew. At once they heard a shot. They threw themselves to the ground. Someone, or something, was shooting at them.

Ed called, "Shorty, are you OK?"

"Yes," came the answer, "don't move."

Another crack of the shotgun. They heard the bullet hit the tree. Then, two more shots.

"Shorty, I think it's Sam. We frightened him coming up the hill. Sam is shooting at us."

"You're right. Let's get behind him."

They went to the other side. It was slow going up. They heard men shouting. "Who is

shooting?'' ''Where is it coming from?''

They got to Sam. He was at the top of the hill, sitting down. His shotgun was next to him. He just sat there and looked at the sky. When they spoke to him, he didn't hear them. They led him back to the horses. It had been too much for him. The old man had cracked up.

Soon, the others started to join them. Ben thought they should call off the hunt. So did everyone. They started home. Ed stayed with Sam. Shorty rode behind them.

Before long, they were close to their campground at the pancake rocks. The moon was high. It looked like a white dish in the sky. On the ground, the grass and trees had wild shapes in the moonlight.

''Sam, you tired?'' Ed asked him. ''Want to rest?''

Sam didn't answer. All the same, Ed decided to let him rest.

''Shorty,'' he called, ''we are going up to the camp. We'll sit a spell on the rocks. Wait for us.''

Shorty said OK.

Ed rode his horse into the clearing. Sam followed. They got off and went up to the top of the rocks. They sat looking into the valley. The moon was overhead. Nothing was said. Sam just looked, seeing nothing. Ed was about to speak. He stopped. He felt something. Something was behind them. His skin went cold. He turned and saw it. A face hanging in the air. A white face, without eyes. It was floating in the air, white as snow, shining in the moonlight.

CHAPTER 5

THE INDIAN

Ed jumped up. His fingers were on his shotgun. He was afraid to speak. Finally, he said, "Who is it?"

The face hung there. Now Ed's eyes got used to the darkness. He could see a body under that face. Someone was standing there.

Sam got up. Ed reached over and pushed Sam's shotgun into the air. He held it there.

"Don't shoot, Sam. It's the old Indian. He has his ghost paint on."

Ed looked at the thing standing there. "You crazy old man. I might have shot you."

The Indian came to these hills every summer. Not for long. He prayed and did his ghost dance. Then he went back to his home.

"Sam, are you OK?"

Sam just looked at the Indian.

"It's all right. Don't shoot." Ed let go of

Sam's shotgun. Sam held it with both hands. He kept it pointed up.

Shorty rode into the clearing. He called to Ed. "Are you OK?"

"Yes. Come up here."

Shorty got to the top. He looked at the Indian. "Who—? What is that?"

"Just an old Indian," Ed told him. "He frightened us."

The Indian had painted his face. But not around his eyes. It was like a mask. Some said he was about eighty years old. The Indian said over a hundred.

Shorty spoke to him. "Old man, we are looking for a mountain lion. Where do we look? It killed a boy."

He was sure the Indian had seen it. Or heard it.

Ed said, "Let's just follow the Indian. Cat sees that mask, it will drop dead."

Sam held his shotgun. His hands started to shake.

"Sam, it's OK," Ed told him.

Shorty spoke to the Indian again. "Old man, the cat is wild," he said.

The white face moved a bit. The mouth opened. It was just a black hole in the white mask. The mask spoke. The hole opened and closed.

"The cat is not wild. The Indian is not wild."

Sam's eyes opened wide. Ed put his hand on Sam's shoulder.

The mask spoke. "Once, Indians and animals lived together, at peace. Then the white man came to this land. He said the

animal was wild. He said the Indian was wild. He killed the buffalo and took the land.

"I come here to pray. I pray the Indian will take back the land. I pray the Indian will live again with the animals.

"The animal is not wild. The cat is not wild."

It happened too fast to stop it. Sam brought his shotgun down and fired. Ed jumped. The shot cracked. The Indian went down. Sam Parker's bullet was in his chest.

Shorty looked at the Indian. He had fixed pads to his feet. He had soft shoes. He had fixed the pads to the bottoms. With each step, he left a paw print in the dirt. The tops of his shoes looked like the cat's feet. They were lined with lion's hair.

Shorty told Ed about it. It was one of the Indian's stories. He believed the feet made him closer to the animals. Like he was a part of the land, Shorty told Ed. That was important.

Shorty said, "Now we know what we saw back there. The Indian was the thing in the dark."

The dead man's body was tied across a horse. Someone led Sam's horse. The old man just sat in the saddle. He was still looking at nothing at all. They rode home.

Heads bowed, some of them were sleeping as they rode. Most of them were sad. No one spoke. It was getting light when they rode out of the hills.

Ed and Shorty rode together. After a while, Ed said, "Two people dead because of that cat."

Shorty didn't speak.

"Another gone mad."

"It's just an animal," Shorty said.

"But look what it's done." Ed was angry.

Shorty took his hat off. The sun was up. It was warm.

"In the first place," he said, "the cat didn't kill the boy just to be killing. It thought the boy was going to take its food away. The lamb that it killed.

"In the second place," he went on, "Sam killed the Indian, not the cat. And Sam didn't go crazy just today. He's had a hard life."

Ed thought about it. A hard life. Shorty said that.

"You're right," he said. "Hard winters that kill the sheep. Hot summers that dry up the land. Bad water that killed Sam's son and his son's wife. And my mother."

Shorty looked up. The sun was getting hotter.

"Another thing," Ed said, "that boy— Sam's grandson—he was the last boy child. The last Parker. That must have killed Sam."

Sam's no good anymore, Shorty thought. He's been beat.

"Maybe the Indian was right," Ed said. "Maybe we should live like they did—50 or 60 years ago. This land beats you down. Maybe it was better before. Maybe white men can't make it here."

Shorty looked at Ed. He said, "The Indian was talking about what is past. About buffalo. Talk about sheep. The land is for the sheep, now. So let's get on with it."

"Poor old man," Ed said softly.

"Which one?"

"Both of them."

After that day, Sam Parker just sat on his front step. Every day he just sat looking at the sky. He never spoke.

They had locked him up for a few months. Then they sent him away. He came home soon after and just sat. He died while Ed was in the war.

CHAPTER **6**

THE FIGHT

Sheep were killed that summer. But no one ever saw the cat. In August once, Ed and Shorty got time to go fishing. They went to their campground.

They were getting fishing line from the well. Shorty was putting his fishing things together. Suddenly, he stopped and stood still. Ed looked at him.

"Don't move," Shorty whispered.

Ed slowly turned his head. Out of the corner of his eye, he saw the cat. It was ten feet away, low on the ground. It was set to spring at them.

Before they could move, it came. Shorty pushed Ed away and ducked behind the well. The cat went over it. It hit Ed and he fell on the ground. He had smashed his head on a rock. He looked up. Shorty stood in front of him. His hunting knife was in his hand.

"Get behind the well," he shouted.

The lion came again. Shorty was down low. As the cat jumped, he stood up fast and knocked its front legs up. He moved and missed the animal's throat. Instead, the knife opened a gash across its chest. The cat jumped away.

Shorty was down. The cat was on him in a second. Its claws were digging into his legs. The cat's mouth got to his neck. Shorty rammed his arm into the cat's mouth. The teeth were digging in. His arm cracked. With his other arm, Shorty used the knife, again and again. He got his legs under the cat and kicked. The cat flew off, but Shorty lost the knife.

Ed got to his feet. The cat came at him. Its front legs hit him. At the same time, Shorty threw a punch from the side. It hit the cat's jaw hard. The animal was shaken. Ed was down. He couldn't believe what was happening. Shorty, in a fight with a lion. It was crazy.

Shorty stood away from Ed. He was in the center of the clearing. His shirt hung from his body. Cuts were all over his chest, back, and arms. Some were very deep. Blood covered him, bright and shining in the sun.

"Wild, are you, cat," he said, "well, I will tame you."

Ed shouted, "Shorty, you can't fight a mountain lion with your hands."

The cat was getting set. Shorty turned his left side to it. Feet wide, he bent over. The cat jumped. Shorty swung from the ground. He hit

like an iron ball. Crack! The cat's back legs dropped in the dirt and dragged.

The cat fell forward and knocked Shorty down. The cat jumped to its feet. Too slow. Shorty threw another punch. Crack! The same jaw. Ed thought that was it for the cat.

The cat stood up again. Ed's mouth hung open. It's wild, he thought. It thinks it's a fighter. He couldn't believe any of it.

The cat was hurt, but not enough to stop. It came again. This time Shorty's punch missed. The cat was on him. Its claws got Shorty's face and shoulders. The two of them rolled and kicked in the dust.

Now, Ed jumped on the animal's back. He hit and bit. The cat jumped away. Ed kicked it. It ran off into the trees. Ed ran after it. He was out of his head. He shouted at it. "You're crazy. You're both crazy. Everyone goes crazy on this land."

Ed tripped and landed in the grass. He beat on the ground. He was crying. "You are all crazy," he said. He lay there. Then he went back to Shorty.

He would never forget. It was the last hour of Shorty's life. Not for many years, not even when he went to war, would he forget. Shorty was sitting on the ground, head down. Some of his skin was torn away. He had a big gash between his shoulder and neck. He cried. His mouth moved. Ed looked at his face. Part of his nose had been torn off.

Tears came to Ed's eyes. The mouth moved again. Ed put his ear closer to that bloody face.

"The knife." It was a low whisper.

"We don't need it, Shorty. The lion's gone."

The mouth moved again. "Kill me."

Ed's eyes opened wide. His mouth dropped open. "No," he cried. "I can't do it."

Ed sat with him for a long time. Then, Shorty died. Ed put him on the ground. He covered him with their coats. Then he carried him down to the truck.

CHAPTER 7

BROKEN JAW

Ed sat shaking in the well. He had thought about all that had happened. It was all three years ago. Today would be the end of it. The cat would kill him, too.

He had been sleeping a little in the well. He couldn't push his legs out. They were stiff and his shoulder hurt. He couldn't stay in the well much longer. He needed a doctor.

The sun was coming up. Anyway, he would be warm soon. He decided to try to stand. It took his all. But he grabbed the wall and pulled himself up. For a second, he blacked out. But he was on his feet. It was hard to see, though. His eyes were not right yet.

The sun came through the trees. It was warm on his face. His head cleared, but he still felt strange. He saw the rocks on the floor of the well. He had been sleeping without rocks on top of him. The cat must have stayed away.

Ed shouted. "Cat, you have to fight me, now. Then we will see who owns this ground."

He was out of his head. He laughed and fell back. The stone wall stopped his fall. He sat on the wall.

Maybe the cat is gone, he thought. The gunpowder scared it off. Maybe it's gone for good. He wondered why it came back. Why did it go after him? No one had seen it. But it was still killing sheep. And it ate garbage. Some big animal got into their garbage. All the time. But no one had seen it.

Something caught his eye. It was outside the well, on the ground. He tried to see it.

"It's Shorty's knife." It's been there three years, he thought. In the grass and dirt.

Holding on, he lifted a leg out of the well. He was shaky.

"Once more, the other leg," he said to himself.

He got the other leg out. On the pancake rocks, the cat was watching him.

He took a step. The knife was right next to him.

"Now, can I pick it up?" he asked himself.

Slowly, he bent over and picked up the knife.

He thought he must be crazy. He couldn't fight the cat. He looked up at the pancake rocks. He saw nothing.

"If Shorty—"

The cat jumped at Ed. It knocked him to the ground. He didn't see it. But he got his arm up and rammed it into the cat's mouth. That's what Shorty did. He felt the jaws close on his arm. The cat cut his face. He hit with the knife. The cat had his arm, but there was no pain. The cat couldn't close its jaw!

He hit again. The knife broke. It came out of his hand. The cat dropped off and ran. The knife had hurt it. But not enough.

Ed was bleeding from the shoulder again. He looked into the well.

"Shorty," he said, breathing hard, *"you broke its jaw.* It couldn't use its teeth."

He reached into the well. He put a handful of snow on his shoulder.

Garbage! For three years the cat had been eating garbage. It couldn't close its jaws. It must have torn me open with its claws, not its teeth, Ed thought.

He spotted a hill of snow. He took short stiff steps. He made it to the snow. He lay in it, packed his shoulder, then passed out. They found him in the snow bank. He was in bed for three weeks.

Summer was almost over when he got back home. Folks were buying cattle now. He was happy to get back to work. His dad needed him.

One day, he drove the truck to the church graveyard. He put wild flowers on Shorty's grave. A simple square stone was at the head. It said:

Jacob Short
1910—1942

CHAPTER **8**

THE LAST HUNT

Summer turned to fall. The land began to cool off. Most of the work was done. John and Ed Winner had more cows now. They were fencing in winter grassland for them. A few men worked for them. They could pay for help, now.

The snows would come soon. Everyone in the valley looked for a good winter. It had to be, they told each other. A winter with little snow maybe. But the cat was still in the valley.

It was killing sheep more often. But it never could eat much. That broken jaw didn't work. The animal had to work hard to tear meat off its kill. It never got enough. So it would have to kill soon again. Or eat garbage. The cat stayed. The only food was in the valley.

One morning, Ed and his dad picked up a sick cow. They drove their truck along the valley. A neighbor told them he had seen the cat. He told them where. Driving back, Ed made up his mind.

"I'm going after it," he told his dad.

John Winner spoke softly. "You spent one night in pain. You almost died. Isn't that enough?"

Ed didn't answer. They were close to home.

His dad asked him to wait. "I'll get five or six men. It's not safe just you going."

"It will be too late. It has to be now," Ed said.

He got his horse. He packed food, water, and a box of shells. He took food for the horse. A small box of gunpowder was in his coat. He put his shotgun in the bag.

"Be careful, son. That cat is big," his dad said.

Behind his saddle, Ed tied a bedroll. He rode out. John Winner called after him, ''You can't bring back the dead.''

''That's not why I'm going,'' Ed called back over his shoulder.

It was true, Ed thought. Shorty's dead. So is the boy. So are the Indian and Sam Parker. But the cat's just an animal, as Shorty said. And you don't get even with an animal.

But the cat has to be stopped. You can't do much about snow and burning sun. But I can stop that cat, he thought. Three years ago, Ben Kincaid said it all. You want the land to grow sheep? Then you have to keep at it, Ben said. Well, Ed thought, just one clean shot.

The cat had been seen halfway up the valley. He found the place. It was still early. Horse and rider went into the hills. Right off, he spotted the cat's prints. He followed them for an hour. The cat was headed for the high country. The trail went up sharply. Hard, rocky ground was coming up. He knew he would see no prints then. He would have to watch for the animal. This time, no surprises, he said to himself.

He took a look around. Below, the valley was far off now. The green had turned yellow in the fall. The horse's feet beat the dirt. Their trail dusted the sunlight. Ed stopped and looked ahead. The trail went to the right, then left, then ahead, higher and higher. They climbed.

The sun went behind the hills. Ed pulled his coat up around his neck. He could smell winter in the cool air. It might even snow tonight, he thought. It didn't matter. The first snow didn't last long. But if it got bad, he would go back.

He kept his horse's head up. He watched as he rode. "No surprises," he said out loud.

The cat could still kill. It could come on him fast. He wouldn't hear it. It came down to one thing: who saw the other—first. He had the shotgun. He wanted just one clean shot.

The horse was climbing. But its front feet were slipping. Ed got off and led the horse. The trail went up. The horse dug in its back feet. It drove forward, then dug in again. The horse worked hard.

Then, the ground got flat. Ed could see the trail. It was even for a long way. On either side the rocks stood like walls. The trail was like a long hallway.

In front, the cat stood in the trail. It was watching them. Ed saw it. He took his shotgun

from the saddlebag. The horse just walked on.
Then it saw the cat, too. It stopped, eyes wide.

Ed dug his feet into the horse. Crack. He
fired the shotgun into the air. The horse shot
forward, fast. Before the cat knew it, the horse
and rider pounded down on it. The cat took off,
running hard. Ed fired the shotgun, once,
twice, again. Bullets hit the rocks near the cat.
Pieces of rock flew at it. The horse was
catching up. The cat tried to jump off the trail.
But the rock walls gave it no footing. It

couldn't get away. The cat turned to face the horse.

The horse pounded down on it. The horse never lost a step. It kept going. Ed pulled the horse's head up hard. He turned it around fast. But the cat ran by. Ed jumped from the horse and fired. Bullet-broken rock hit the cat's feet. In one great jump, the cat went over the wall of rock. It was free.

Ed held the horse's head. He rubbed its face.

"Nice going, horse," he said. "Cat's on the run now."

They rested a few minutes. Ed put bullets in the shotgun. They rode on, climbing again. A wind came up. It started to snow. Ed put his head down. The snow fell heavily for an hour. Horse and rider were in the high country now. They were a small dot against the white snow. Now and then, Ed fired the shotgun into the air. The noise would keep the cat moving.

After a while the snow let up. Ed could see in front. But it was almost dark. He spotted the old shack. Years ago the shack was used by miners. He decided to spend the night there.

Ed headed the horse for it. It had almost stopped snowing. Good, Ed thought. It was not too deep. He could follow the cat's trail in the snow. And it wouldn't slow the horse. Tonight, he would sleep in the shack. In the morning, he could start out again.

He came closer to the shack. The horse stopped. Ed dug his feet in its side. It took a few more steps. Then, it stopped again. It was looking at the shack. The door hung open. Ed got off the horse. He looked around. Behind the shack was the opening to the mine. The cat could be in either place. He fired the shotgun into the air. Nothing happened.

Ed got the gunpowder from his coat. He took it out of the box. It was inside some paper. He put half of it back into the box. He put that into his coat. Carefully, he walked to the shack, shotgun pointed at the open door.

There was not a sound. He got to the door. He lit the paper around the gunpowder. It burned slowly. Then he threw it into the shack. It flashed up on the dirt floor. The flash lit up the inside. But Ed saw nothing. White smoke came out the door. Ed got a flashlight from his saddle bag. He went into the shack. Nothing.

He led the horse toward the shack. He tried to get it to go in. The horse wouldn't go in. The cat's been here, all right, Ed thought. The horse was still afraid. Ed cracked it on the behind. It went in. He tied the door closed.

There was a table inside. Made from wooden boxes. Ed broke it up. He threw the wood into an old iron stove.

"Let's see if the stove works," he said to the horse.

He lit it. It was smoky, but the shack warmed up.

Ed took the saddle off the horse. He gave it food and water. Then he cooked food for himself. He ate, then he laid out his sleeping bag. He got into the bag. The horse's head moved up. Its ears were up. The cat's out there, Ed thought.

He thought of another night. It was in France and his first night in battle. He and other men had waited in the dark. Then, the noise came. They couldn't hear. Shells blowing up around them. Flashes of light from guns. Men shouting. Men hit. Men screaming. He had fired his gun. But he couldn't hear it above the other noise.

The cat comes and never makes a sound. He asked himself which was worse. Which is more frightening. The war, or the cat. Both were very bad. No, he thought. It's better to fight the cat. You just have to spot it, before it spots you. And then? Just one clean shot, he said to himself.

CHAPTER 9

ONE CLEAN SHOT

Ed went to sleep. It was getting light when he woke. He ate. He gave the horse food. He tied his bedroll to the saddle.

"Time to go, horse," he said.

He led it toward the opening to the mine. The horse followed, then stopped. Ed pulled. The horse wouldn't move. The cat is in the mine, Ed said to himself. He went closer. The cat's footprints led into the mine. But not out again!

Ed got the flashlight and went in. Grasses grew from the walls. He pulled some of it down. It was dry. He lit it and threw it ahead. Wind sent the smoke deep into the mine. He turned his flashlight on. The mine didn't go far. Its roof had fallen in years ago. But there was a small hole in the rocks. At the back. It led deeper into the mine. He put the rest of the gunpowder there. Again, a burning flash and

some white smoke. Then, nothing. Ed went back to the horse.

Getting on the horse, he saw the smoke. It was up the hill, above the mine opening. It was coming out of the ground. White smoke. The gunpowder smoke, he thought. It went into that small hole. It went deeper, then up. Now, Ed knew. The cat had another way out.

He slipped the shotgun into the bag.
He rode up the hill fast. Halfway up he got off the horse. He ran to the white smoke. Sure enough. He saw the cat's footprints. There was the hole. The cat had come out this way.

"I let you get away, cat," he said.

Ed thought it was the luckiest animal around. Talk about nine lives of a cat. How can anyone fight a cat like that? Just then, the ground fell from under his feet. Rocks, trees, and snow just dropped into the earth. The mine was falling in under him. Ed grabbed for something, anything. He fell.

He landed on a small tree. It broke his fall. The snow helped, too. He was OK. He found his hat. Then he made his way out. Rocks and old wood were everywhere. He looked back. It was no longer a mine. Just a gash in the side of the mountain.

He followed the cat's trail all morning. He was on flat even ground. The sun was bright. He could see a long way in front of him. The cat showed itself once. But it was far off.

Once before, Ed had been up in this country. He remembered it. He would come to a large, flat field. There were no rocks or trees on it. It was like a lake. Smooth and flat, but it turned up a little at the outside. There was a small hill. The cat would have to cross it.

Ed dug into the horse. It took off fast. It wanted to run. Snow flew under it. Its legs reached and pounded. The wind hurt Ed's face, but he let the horse go all out.

Soon, it tired. Ed got off. The animal was wet from the run. He took the cover off his bedroll. With that, he rubbed the horse dry. Now, they walked.

Ed kept it up. A run, then a walk. They got to the field. Snow covered it. It was like a white lake. And they were in time. The cat was walking across the center of the field. It was headed for the other side. It looked white, too. It was hard to see against the snow. At times, Ed couldn't see it. It was too far away. He would have to get closer.

He held the horse's head. "Once more, horse. We can win." Ed said to it. He got on and took his shotgun out. He held it in both hands. The horse knew what to do. It took off strong, down to the field. It picked up speed. Feet were reaching, pounding, flying. Snow flew in a storm behind. Ed felt the animal's power. His coat was blowing like a flag.

The cat heard the horse. It turned. It looked for a second—a second it lost for escape. And it ran. But its run was not strong. It was the weak one, now.

Ed pulled up the horse. Its legs stiffened. Its feet dug in fast. Before it stopped, he jumped. He rolled over in the snow. He had his shotgun in his hands. He aimed. His hands shook. He put his head down. He waited.

The cat slowed and walked easily. It reached the other side of the field. It would have an easy climb now. Ed looked along the side of the shotgun. The cat walked out of the field. It started up the hill. Ed told himself to wait. Wait until it reaches the top. Then, he would see it against the bright sky. He was ready.

The cat reached the top. It stood with the blue sky at its back. Head up, it looked. Ed took careful aim. The cat was at the end of his life. It had lost.

Ed pulled the trigger. Crack. The cat's head jumped up. Its legs danced. Its dead body dropped like a rock on the ground.

One clean shot, Ed thought. He walked to the spot. The horse followed. Ed looked at the dead lion. It looked like it was sleeping. Shorty was right, he thought. It's only an animal.